WELCOME TO
PASSPORT TO READING
A beginning reader's ticket to a brand-new world!

Every book in this program is designed to build read-along and read-alone skills, level by level, through engaging and enriching stories. As the reader turns each page, he or she will become more confident with new vocabulary, sight words, and comprehension.

These PASSPORT TO READING levels will help you choose the perfect book for every reader.

READING TOGETHER
Read short words in simple sentence structures together to begin a reader's journey.

READING OUT LOUD
Encourage developing readers to sound out words in more complex stories with simple vocabulary.

READING INDEPENDENTLY
Newly independent readers gain confidence reading more complex sentences with higher word counts.

READY TO READ MORE
Readers prepare for chapter books with fewer illustrations and longer paragraphs.

This book features sight words from the educator-supported Dolch Sight Words List. This encourages the reader to recognize commonly used vocabulary words, increasing reading speed and fluency.

For more information, please visit passporttoreadingbooks.com.

Enjoy the journey!

Little, Brown and Company

Hachette Book Group
1290 Avenue of the Americas, New York, NY 10104
Visit us at lb-kids.com

Little, Brown and Company is a division of Hachette Book Group, Inc.
The Little, Brown name and logo are trademarks of Hachette Book Group, Inc.

The publisher is not responsible for websites (or their content)
that are not owned by the publisher.

First Edition: April 2017

Library of Congress Control Number: 2016947537

ISBN 978-0-316-54815-1

10   9   8   7   6   5   4   3   2   1

CW

Printed in the United States of America

HiT entertainment

Passport to Reading titles are leveled by independent reviewers applying the standards developed by Irene Fountas and Gay Su Pinnell in *Matching Books to Readers: Using Leveled Books in Guided Reading*, Heinemann, 1999.

Adapted by Lauren Forte

Based on the episode "Car Wash"

written by Simon Davies

LITTLE, BROWN AND COMPANY
New York   Boston

Attention, Bob the Builder fans!
Look for these words
when you read this book.
Can you spot them all?

main frame

brushes

button

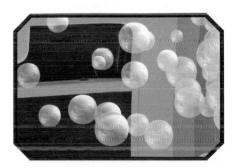

bubbles

Bob and his crew were ready to work. "Today we are building a new car wash for Curtis's garage!" Bob said.

Roley had to make sure
the tarmac was smooth.

"Roley likes to do his jobs perfectly!"
said Muck.

"He likes to do them a bit too perfectly,"
said Lofty.

Curtis wanted to see how
the team was doing.

Finally Roley said the tarmac
was just right.
The team cheered!

Just then Phillip drove in with
Mr. Bentley and Mayor Madison.

"Are you open?" Mr. Bentley asked.

"Not yet," said Wendy.

"Phillip will be washed first when
we are ready!"

The team was running late.
"We need to make up time,"
Bob said.

The team got started.

The main frame was built.

The water was connected.

Bob and Leo placed the brushes.

They had to test the car wash.

"You do the honors, Curtis," said Wendy.

She pointed to the green button.

The car wash worked perfectly!

"Now I can open the garage," said Curtis.

But Roley was worried.

"I think I should roll the tarmac
once more," he told Bob.

"I will do another test," said Leo. But Roley was already smoothing the tarmac again.

Leo yelled at Rolcy to stop.
He should not roll when
the car wash is running!
But Roley kept rolling.

Roley was too close to the brushes.

He backed up...

and crashed into the main frame.

"It is all my fault!" cried Roley.

"Is there anything we
can do, Bob?" Curtis asked.
"Of course there is!" Bob said.

Bob was sure they could fix the car wash!
"Okay everyone, can we fix it?" he asked.
"YES, WE CAN!" the team said.

Leo reconnected the water.

Lofty reattached the brushes.

Everyone else fixed the main frame.

Phillip drove in again for his wash.

Mayor Madison rolled down her window.

"We are in a hurry!" she told Curtis.

The brushes and rollers
started to spin around Phillip.

"Wait! Close your window!"
Wendy warned.
But it was too late.

Soapy bubbles filled the car.
Mayor Madison and Mr. Bentley
were soaked!

"Look on the bright side," Bob said.

"At least Phillip is clean."

"Sparkling, sir," Phillip said.

And he really was.